Fishing

The World's Greatest Fishing Spots and Techniques

by Paul Mason

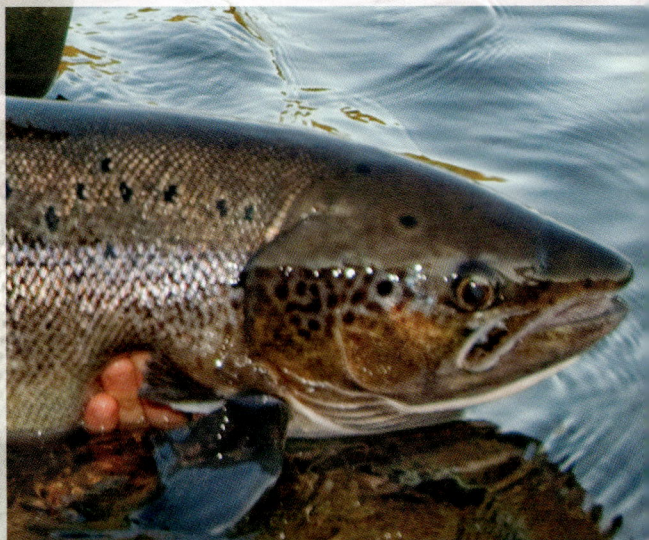

CAPSTONE PRESS
a capstone imprint

Edge Books are published by
Capstone Press, a Capstone imprint,
151 Good Counsel Drive, P.O. Box 669,
Mankato, Minnesota 56002.
www.capstonepub.com

First published 2011
Copyright © 2011 A & C Black
Publishers Limited

Produced for A & C Black by
Monkey Puzzle Media Ltd,
11 Chanctonbury Road,
Hove BN3 6EL, UK

032011
006117ACF11

The right of Paul Mason to be identified as
the author of this Work has been asserted by
him in accordance with the Copyright, Designs,
and Patents Act 1988.

Library of Congress Cataloging-in-Publication
Data
Mason, Paul, 1967-
  Fishing : the world's greatest fishing spots
and techniques / by Paul Mason.
      p. cm. -- (Passport to world sports)
  Includes index.
  ISBN 978-1-4296-6864-4 (library binding)
 1. Fishing--Juvenile literature. 2. Fishing--
Guidebooks--Juvenile literature. I. Title.
II. Series.

 SH445.M233 2011
 639.2--dc22

2011003315

Editor: Dan Rogers
Design: Mayer Media
Picture research: Lynda Lines

This book is produced using paper that
is made from wood grown in managed,
sustainable forests. It is natural, renewable,
and recyclable. The logging and manufacturing
processes conform to the environmental
regulations of the country of origin.

Picture acknowledgements
Alamy pp. 1 (Steve Bly), 6 (Aurora Photos), 8
(Peter Brown), 9 (David Moore), 10 (Aurora
Photos), 14 (Philip Quirk), 16 (Rob Watkins), 17
(Chris Cheadle), 18 (Ryan Bonneau), 19 (Ryan
Bonneau), 20 (Stock Connection Distribution),
21 (Steve Bly), 22 (RJH Catalog), 25 (Larry
Larsen); Corbis p. 11 (AlaskaStock); Louisiana
Office of Tourism pp. 12, 13; MPM Images
p. 28; Nature Picture Library p. 29 (Jeff
Vanuga); Photolibrary pp. 5 (Aflo Foto
Agency), 23 (All Canada Photos); Rex Features
pp. 4 (Hot Stock), 15 (Ian Bird), 24; Wikimedia
pp. 7, 26; Zice Holidays p. 27. Compass rose
artwork on front cover and inside pages by
iStockphoto. Map artwork
by MPM Images.

The front cover shows a fly fisherman catching
a trout in Colorado (Photolibrary/Hot Stock).

Every effort has been made to contact copyright
holders of material reproduced in this book.
Any omissions will be rectified in subsequent
printings if notice is given to the publishers.

SAFETY ADVICE

Don't attempt any of the
activities or techniques
in this book without the
guidance of a qualified
instructor.

CONTENTS

It's a Fish-Filled World

You're slowly winding in the reel, and suddenly there's a tug on your fishing rod. The line starts to zip outward—a fish! And a big one, by the feel of it. But what exactly is on the end of your line? You'll only find out by using all your skill and reeling in the fish without losing it.

A bass fights to free itself from an angler's line. Once it had been reeled in, this fish was released back into the wild.

THE SECRET LANGUAGE OF FISHING

lures artificial baits, made of plastic or metal
breakable able to be pulled apart into smaller pieces

THE WORLD OF FISHING

You can go fishing almost anywhere you find water. People fish in freezing Arctic seas, warm Indian lakes, fast-flowing rivers in the Rockies, Andes and Alps, and in every one of the world's seas and oceans. They have developed all kinds of different fishing gear, too. If it seems confusing, don't worry! There is plenty of advice on equipment in this book.

THE WORLD'S BEST FISHING SPOTS

Imagine you could go fishing anywhere in the world. Where would you go? Where are the absolute BEST places to fish? This book will tell you what you need to know, so just turn the page to find out more.

Ideal fishing kit for a beginner. A rod and reel like these can be used for both float fishing and spinning.

Technical: Fishing equipment

There are thousands of different combinations of rods, reels, lines, and tackle that you can use for fishing. These are the main different kinds:

River fishing:

• Many people use a "float rod," a light rod about 10 feet (3 meters) long.

• The most common reel is a fixed-spool reel.

• Thin nylon line and a variety of floats, hooks, and baits, depending on what you want to catch.

Sea fishing:

• Beach-casting rods are usually about 13 feet (4 meters) long. Boat-fishing rods are shorter, and more sturdy.

• Fixed-spool reels are most common.

• Thin nylon line and a variety of hooks, baits, and **lures**.

Game fishing:

• Fly-fishing or spinning rods are light and are usually about 9 feet (2.75 meters) long.

• Fixed-spool reels for spinning; special fly reels for fly-fishing.

• Thin nylon line and spinning lures for spinning; thicker lines and flies for fly fishing.

For a beginner, the best fishing kit is probably a fixed-spool reel, a light, **breakable** rod about 9 feet (2.75 meters) long, and a variety of lures and floats.

River Arno

RIVER ARNO
Location: Florence, Italy
Type of fishing: river (bank)
Difficulty level: 1 of 5
Best season: May to June and September to October

Just to prove that you can find great fishing almost anywhere, our first stop is in the middle of the ancient city of Florence, Italy. Here you can cast a line into the river, as the bells of the thousand-year-old church towers ring out in the morning.

Tip from a Local
The giant catfish caught in the Arno in 2007 (see opposite) was hooked using a bait of old bread.

TECHNIQUE
Tying a hook or weight to the end of a line

You'll never catch a fish unless your hook is tied on securely! This is a simple, reliable way to tie a hook or weight to the end of a fishing line:

1. Thread the line through the eye of the hook/weight, and make a loop on the end of the line.

2. Turn the end of the line over the section of line leading from the tip of

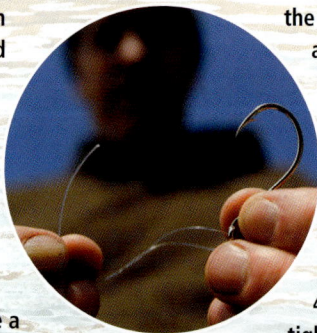

the rod to the hook/weight, and back through the loop. Repeat five or six times.

3. Pull the line tight. Take care not to catch your fingers or thumb on the tip of the hook. It's easily done!

4. Just before it's really tight, wet the knot with spit or water. Then pull it tight. You're now ready to hook a fish!

This weir across the River Arno is one of the city's most popular fishing spots.

If you like the River Arno ...
you could also try:
- River Aire, Leeds, England
- Hudson River, New York

FISHING THE RIVER ARNO

The best fishing spots are right in the city center, downstream from the market. Legends tell of a giant fish that stalks the Arno, and in 2007 a huge catfish weighing 66 pounds (30 kilograms) and 5.6 feet (1.7 meters) long was caught. The fish was released back into the river, and it's still there, waiting to be caught again.

ESSENTIAL INFORMATION

Fishing is best here in the spring and autumn. Fish for catfish, goldfish, and crucian carp.

Fishing equipment: A simple reel and breakable rod are ideal. Ask in local **tackle shops** for bait.

Clothing: In spring, summer, and autumn, light clothing is fine (with a jacket if necessary). Winters can be cold, especially by the river.

Dungeness Beach

DUNGENESS BEACH
Location: Kent, England
Type of fishing: sea (beach)
Difficulty level: 1.5 of 5
Best season: September to January

At first sight, Dungeness might not appear to be a very attractive place to fish. It's a flat, gloomy **spit** of shingle that sticks out into the English Channel. Worse, there's a nuclear power station perched on the end of it. So why come here? Because you might catch some BIG fish!

FISHING DUNGENESS BEACH

Dungeness is one of the few places where you can still catch big cod from the beach. Cod of more than 22 pounds (10 kilograms) are occasionally reeled in. But you might find almost anything on the end of your line here, including sea bass, whiting, and all kinds of flatfish.

Tip from a Local

If you are fishing for cod the best bait is bits of peeler crab. Cod can't resist them!

The shingle bank at Dungeness is crowded with anglers hoping to land a massive cod.

ESSENTIAL INFORMATION

Early autumn is a good time to visit Dungeness. You have a chance of good weather (or at least not freezing weather), and all kinds of fish will be biting.

Fishing equipment: For cod, use a beach-casting rod that can make long casts. For bass, the biggest fish are usually within about 50 feet (15 meters) of the shore. **Live bait** is best.

Clothing: It can get chilly, so always make sure you've got a warm jacket, hat, and gloves.

If you like Dungeness Beach ...

you could also try:
• Orford Ness, England
• Skarnsundet Fjordsenter, Norway
• Cape Cod, Massachusetts

TECHNIQUE
Beach casting

The rod whips through as this angler makes a long, two-handed cast from the beach.

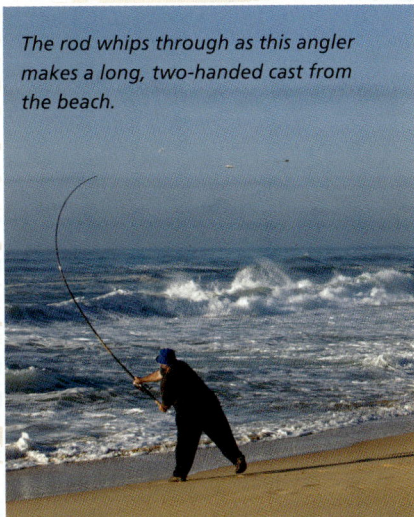

When fishing from a beach, you may have to cast a long way out. Here's a technique to try (these instructions are for someone right-handed, so reverse them if you're left-handed).

1. Grip the rod with both hands, turn to the right, and point your left shoulder where you want to cast. Swing the rod backward until it is pointing behind you, and the weight is lying on the ground.

2. Turn your head to look where you want to cast, then firmly and smoothly pull the rod up and forward. Twist your body around to the left, like a baseball hitter, as you cast.

3. Pull down with your left arm and push forward with your right, to add power to the cast.

Experts can cast over 330 feet (100 meters) this way. That gets their bait into very deep water!

9

Fort Peck Lake

You couldn't make a list of the world's best places to fish without including Montana. Expert fly fishermen head here to fish in the fast-flowing rivers. But for a beginner, Fort Peck Lake is a perfect place to try spinning for all kinds of fish.

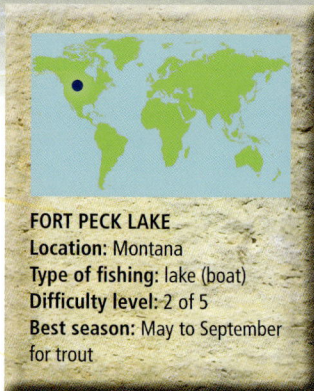

FORT PECK LAKE
Location: Montana
Type of fishing: lake (boat)
Difficulty level: 2 of 5
Best season: May to September for trout

If you like Fort Peck Lake ...
you could also try:
- Lake Nasser, Egypt
- Loch Katrine, Scotland

FISHING FORT PECK LAKE

There are more than 50 different species of fish swimming about in Fort Peck Lake. They include walleye, northern pike, salmon, smallmouth bass, and trout. Of these, trout is one of the most exciting to catch. Trout fight hard when hooked, and anglers need skill and patience to reel them in.

Montana's rivers and beautiful landscapes make it a must-visit destination for anglers. This young girl has caught a trout using fly-fishing gear.

Smile for the camera! He probably doesn't feel much like smiling, but this trout is about to be released back into the river. That should cheer him up.

TECHNIQUE
Landing a fish

ESSENTIAL INFORMATION

As the lake is 134 miles (216 kilometers) long, and steep-sided in places, the best fishing is from a boat. Be careful not to hook your fellow anglers when casting!

Fishing equipment: Use a standard 9-foot (2.75-meter) spinning rod, a fixed-spool reel containing 8 **pound** (3.64 kilogram) **test** line, and a selection of spinning lures.

Clothing: Dress for the season, but always be aware that storms can develop suddenly on the lake.

Once you have caught a fish, you need to "land" it—bring it safely to shore, and remove the hook from its mouth.

1. Once there is only as much line out as the length of your rod, stop reeling in. So, for a 9-foot (2.75-meter) rod, stop reeling when there are 9 feet (2.75 meters) of line stretching from the tip of the rod.

2. Lift the rod into the air, which will guide the fish toward you. Be ready to let out some line if it makes a last-gasp escape attempt!

3. Guide the fish into your landing net, and put down the rod. Grip the fish firmly but not too hard, ideally with a pair of **lip grippers**.

4. Remove the hook. You might need to use a degorger (a special blunt blade with a notched tip) if the hook is deep inside the fish.

Grand Isle Tarpon Rodeo

The Grand Isle Tarpon Rodeo is the oldest fishing contest in the United States. It began in 1928, and today has become one of the biggest, most fun fishing events anywhere. The fishing contest is combined with a music festival, and the usual Grand Isle population of about 1,500 people grows to 20,000 or more.

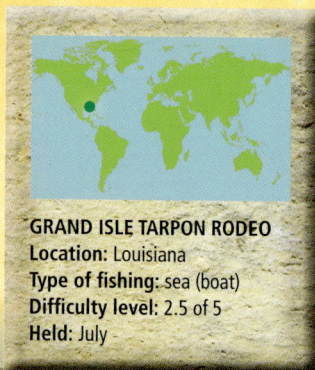

GRAND ISLE TARPON RODEO
Location: Louisiana
Type of fishing: sea (boat)
Difficulty level: 2.5 of 5
Held: July

The weigh-in at the end of a day's fishing during the Grand Isle Tarpon Rodeo

TARPON FISHING

Tarpon is one of the greatest saltwater **game fish**. It is also called the Silver King. The most exciting ways to catch tarpon are fly fishing and spinning. It is tricky to **set** a hook in a tarpon's mouth, which is so hard that some anglers say it is like concrete. These fish are incredibly strong and, once hooked, can sometimes fight for hours to escape.

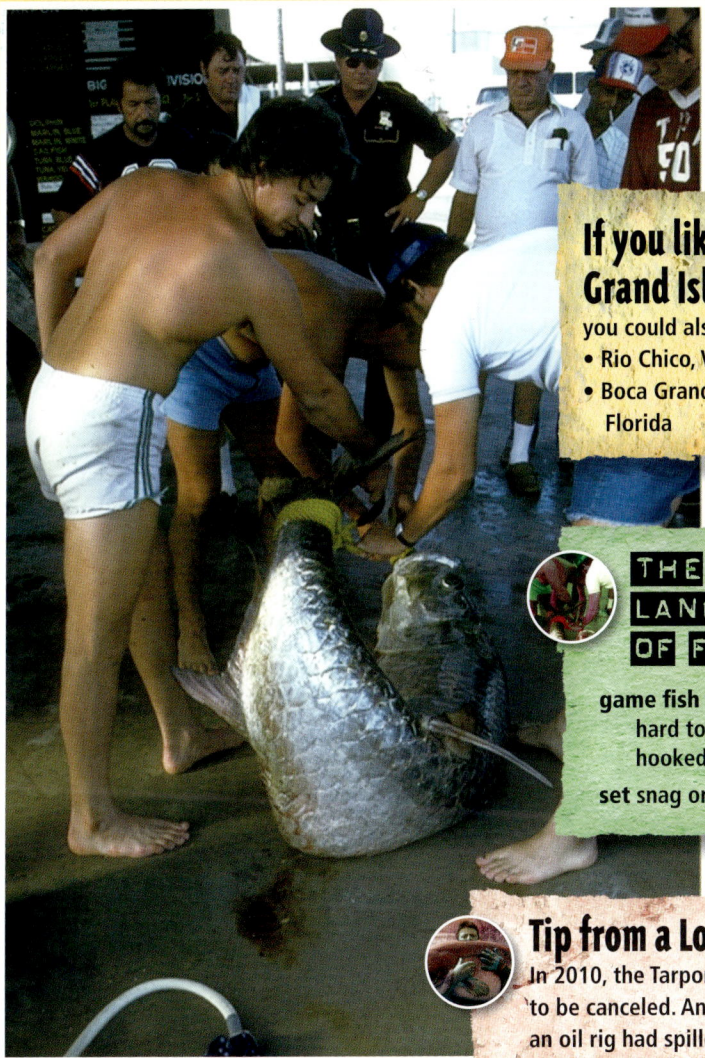

Tarpon can grow extremely large. A whopper like this one would fight hard and be extremely tricky to land.

If you like the Grand Isle Rodeo ...
you could also try:
• Rio Chico, Venezuela
• Boca Grande Pass, Florida

THE SECRET LANGUAGE OF FISHING

game fish fish that fight hard to escape when hooked

set snag or catch

Tip from a Local
In 2010, the Tarpon Rodeo had to be canceled. An accident at an oil rig had spilled almost 5 million barrels of oil into the Gulf of Mexico. The effects made it impossible to hold the Rodeo.

THE TARPON RODEO

The Tarpon Rodeo fishing starts at sunrise on Thursday morning, and the scales weighing fish close at 6 p.m. on Sunday. The big competition is for whoever can land the largest tarpon.

There's a big prize, too. In 2007, the winner got a new boat! There are also competitions for 27 other kinds of fish, including the famous, hard-fighting blue marlin, red snapper, and speckled trout.

Sydney Harbour

Sydney Harbour is one of the world's most amazing places. The 152 miles (244 kilometers) of shoreline includes beautiful beaches, city-center piers, steep cliffs, and wooded coast. The harbor offers pretty much every kind of fishing (apart from ice fishing!).

SYDNEY HARBOUR
Location: New South Wales, Australia
Type of fishing: sea (boat and shore)
Difficulty level: 2.5 of 5
Best season: all year round

Sydney Harbour's many wooden piers provide excellent fishing spots. You can drop your line straight into deep water where the bigger fish are lurking.

Tip from a Local

The best time to fish is early in the morning, on a **turning tide**. Later on, boats criss-crossing the harbor will have scared the fish.

If you like Sydney Harbour ...

you could also try:
- Poole Harbour, England
- Halifax Harbour, Canada

Information: Extreme fishing

Many good fishing spots have become increasingly busy. This makes it harder to catch fish and less peaceful. In response, some anglers have started fishing from hard-to-reach places. This has become known as extreme fishing.

• Extreme fishing sometimes requires a long hike. For example, some trips to catch mahseer (see pages 26 and 27) require several days of walking and camping.

• Some anglers have started abseiling down cliffs to get to isolated fishing spots.

• In the 2000s, anglers in Australia and New Zealand started using high-speed jet skis and waverunners to race out to ocean fisheries. The craze soon began to spread around the world.

Each of these is extremely dangerous, and should only be attempted by expert anglers accompanied by a guide.

THE SECRET LANGUAGE OF FISHING

turning tide time when the tide changes direction

These anglers are perched on the edge of a seawater swimming pool at Avalon, north of Sydney. At least the barriers will give them something to hang on to if a wave tries to wash them away!

Fishing Sydney Harbour

It is possible to fish from the shore, but using a boat will make it easier to move on if the fish aren't biting. Look for quiet spots without too much boat traffic, where deep water becomes shallower. On any given day you might hook Australian bass, bream, kingfish, trevally, bonito, tuna—or even a marlin or a shark.

Essential information

The fishing is good in the harbor all year round. The size and number of fish you can keep is limited on some species.

Fishing equipment: Use a boat rod or a breakable spinning rod, depending on how you are fishing, plus a fixed-spool reel and a variety of baits and lures.

Clothing: The sun is always strong here, even on dull days, so cover up. A warm jacket can be useful, especially in the early morning or evening.

Mull

Mull is an angler's paradise. It is a beautiful, mist-shrouded island off the coast of Scotland. The rivers and **lochs** contain wild trout, and the deep seas off Mull are famous for producing some of the biggest fish ever caught in Britain.

MULL
Location: Western Isles, Scotland
Type of fishing: all kinds
Difficulty level: 2.5 of 5
Best season: May to October

SEA FISHING OFF MULL

Much of Mull's coast is made up of high cliffs, so the best way to fish in the ocean is from a boat. In the Sound of Mull (between Mull and the mainland) some real giants are lurking. In 1986 the biggest skate ever caught in the United Kingdom was landed. It weighed 226.6 pounds (103 kilograms). The Sound is also a great place to fish for sea bass.

The steep cliffs of northern Mull allow anglers to try for deep-sea fish from land. They're no fun if you're scared of heights, though!

If you like Mull ...

you could also try:
- Vancouver Island, Canada
- Cairns, Australia
- Kona, Hawaii

THE SECRET LANGUAGE OF FISHING

loch Scottish lake

TECHNIQUE
Boat fishing

Fishing from a boat uses different techniques to fishing from shore. The rods are shorter and stronger, because deep-sea fish may be heavy!

These guys have hooked some pretty big fish. Deep-sea fish are often larger and stronger than those found closer to shore.

ESSENTIAL INFORMATION

Scotland can be wet at any time of year, and in the winter it also gets cold and stormy. The most enjoyable times of year for fishing are probably spring and autumn.

Fishing equipment: A standard boat rod and a fixed-spool or special boat reel are best, plus tackle for whatever you're fishing for.

Clothing: Dress warm and dry, whatever the time of year.

1. Let your line go freely over the side of the boat. Just dangle it. There's no need to cast.

2. Wait until you feel the line go slack. This means the weight at the end has hit the bottom.

3. Reel in slightly until you can feel the weight tugging on the line once more. Now let tiny bits of line out until you feel the weight resting on the bottom.

Set your hooks and bait as far up or down the line as you think the fish will be feeding. For bottom-feeders, for example, the hooks should be at the same height as the weight.

Ascension Bay

ASCENSION BAY
Location: Yucatan, Mexico
Type of fishing: sea (shallow water)
Difficulty level: 3 of 5
Best season: February to June

After a fishing trip to Mull (see pages 16 and 17), you'll probably need to warm up! Where better than the sunny, warm waters of Ascension Bay in Mexico? As well as having great weather, this is a place that has REALLY great fishing.

FISHING ASCENSCION BAY

The most popular type of fishing here is fly fishing. You can fish from a **skiff** or just by wading out into the shallow water. The Bay has many shallow **lagoons** where you can catch bonefish and tarpon. Both these fish fight hard when hooked, and they are thought to be among the world's most exciting to catch.

A kayak is a great way to get around the shallow waters of Ascension Bay.

If you like Ascension Bay ...
you could also try:
- **Lower Biscayne Bay, Florida**
- **Rio Colorado, Costa Rica**

Tip from a Local
If standing in the sea to fish, wear long, quick-drying pants. They will protect you from stinging "water fleas."

Fly casting

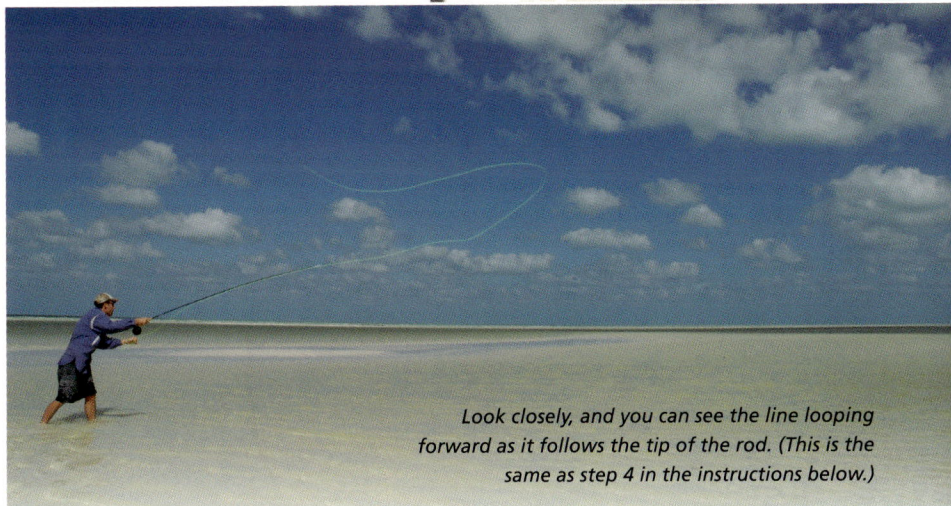

Look closely, and you can see the line looping forward as it follows the tip of the rod. (This is the same as step 4 in the instructions below.)

ESSENTIAL INFORMATION

Fishing using nets is banned in Ascension Bay, which is partly why the waters are so teeming with fish.

Fishing equipment: Use a 9 to 10-foot (2.75 to 3-meter) fly rod. Strong, heavy line to make casting easier on windy days.

Clothing: The sun is strong, so cover up with a hat, long sleeves, and pants. Always wear eye protection when fly fishing.

THE SECRET LANGUAGE OF FISHING

skiff small, wide boat that can float in very shallow water

lagoon large area of shallow water

The best way to learn fly casting is in the middle of a big, grassy field, with no hook attached to the end of the line. It's safest for everyone!

1. Step backward until about 16 feet (5 meters) of line is stretched out in front of you with the rod tip on the ground.

2. Keeping your wrist rigid, lift the rod to about a 10 o'clock position (if seen from the side). The line should begin to lift smoothly off the ground.

3. Smoothly continue to accelerate the rod backward, until it is at the 12 o'clock position. The line will start to snake through the air behind you.

4. When the weight of the line pulls the rod tip backward, bring the rod forward again. The line will follow back through the air and stretch out in front of you.

5. Stop the rod at about 10 o'clock, and let the line settle on the ground.

19

Door Peninsula

The Door Peninsula juts out into the waters of Lake Michigan. To the west is the strip of water known as Green Bay. The little creeks, inlets, and bays on this side of the Door Peninsula are an excellent place to try catching one of North America's favorite fish— the smallmouth bass.

DOOR PENINSULA
Location: Wisconsin
Type of fishing: lake (boat)
Difficulty level: 3 of 5
Best season: May and June

SMALLMOUTH BASS AND THE DOOR PENINSULA

Smallmouth bass are popular with anglers because, when hooked, the fish fights hard against being landed. Some anglers say that for its weight it fights harder than any other fish. Some of the best smallmouth fishing is on the Green Bay coast near the town of Sturgeon Bay. There are also good spots between Egg Harbor and Fish Creek.

A smallmouth bass takes the lure. The angler on the boat is in for an exciting battle as he tries to land this fierce little fish.

Tip from a Local

If you're visiting in summer, bring some insect repellent. The mosquitoes can be vicious!

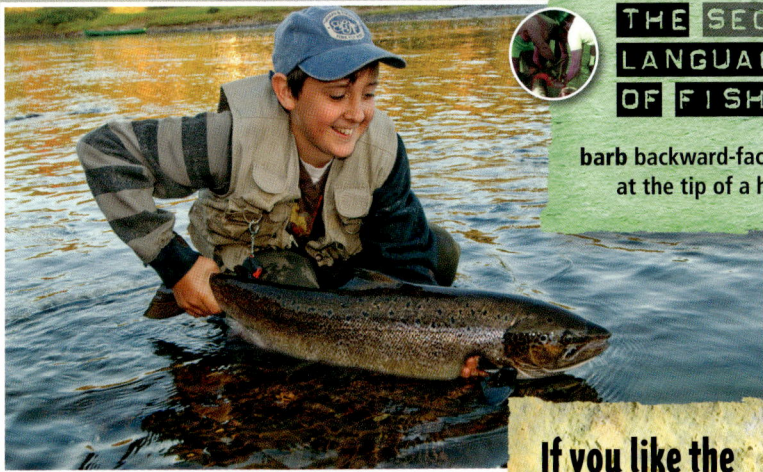

Imagine catching a salmon as long as your arm! This boy is about to let his fish slip back into the water.

THE SECRET LANGUAGE OF FISHING

barb backward-facing spine at the tip of a hook

If you like the Door Peninsula ...

you could also try:
- **Lake Powell, Utah/Arizona**
- **French Creek, Pennsylvania**

TECHNIQUE
Catch-and-release fishing

Many anglers use catch-and-release techniques to make sure that fish numbers do not decline too much.

• Do not use hooks with **barbs**, as these damage a fish's mouth when it is being unhooked. Barbless hooks may even allow you to release a fish without removing it from the water.

• Land fish as quickly as possible. Otherwise, they may be so exhausted that they cannot swim away even after being released.

• Handle fish as little as possible in the dry air. Wiping the slime off a fish's scales with your hands is not good for its health.

• If the fish is tired, try "swimming" it back and forth in the water, while gently cradling it in your hand. This may give it enough oxygen to start moving again.

ESSENTIAL INFORMATION

Although it's possible to fish from the shore or by wading, the best way to fish off the Door Peninsula is probably by boat.

Fishing equipment: Smallmouth bass can be caught using fly, spinning, or bait equipment.

Clothing: Dress for the season. If wading, a pair of warm waders will make the sometimes-chilly waters of Lake Michigan more comfortable.

Kristiinankaupunki

There can't be too many world-famous fishing spots where you have to wear a survival suit! The Gulf of Bothnia, between Finland and Sweden, is one of them—at least in winter. Here, the big attraction for anglers is the area's world-famous sea pike.

KRISTIINANKAUPUNKI
Location: Gulf of Bothnia, Finland
Type of fishing: sea (boat)
Difficulty level: 3.5 of 5
Best season: May, September to December

FISHING KRISTIINANKAUPUNKI

Many kinds of fish swim in the icy waters of the Gulf. They include whitefish, zander, grayling, salmon, sea trout, and perch (which can be caught in winter through a hole drilled in the ice). But *you're* coming here to fly fish or spin for BIG pike—one of the meanest, toughest fish around. If you're lucky, you might hook one of 22 pounds (10 kilograms) or more.

Tip from a Local

This is one area where you'll definitely need to hire a local fishing guide. These waters are rocky and hazardous.

In winter pike can be caught using nets dropped through holes in the ice.

Playing a fish

If you like Kristiinankaupunki ...

you could also try:
- Prince William Sound, Alaska
- Chiloé Island, Chile

This trout will put up quite a fight before it can be reeled in.

ESSENTIAL INFORMATION

The best time of year for pike fishing is in September and October, as the water begins to get colder.

Fishing equipment: For pike, the most important bit of kit is wire **traces**, as pike will bite through nylon. A rod and line strong enough to land a fish of 22 pounds (10 kilograms) or more is also required.

Clothing: Mosquitoes can be a problem in summer, so stay covered up. In winter, full survival gear is usually needed.

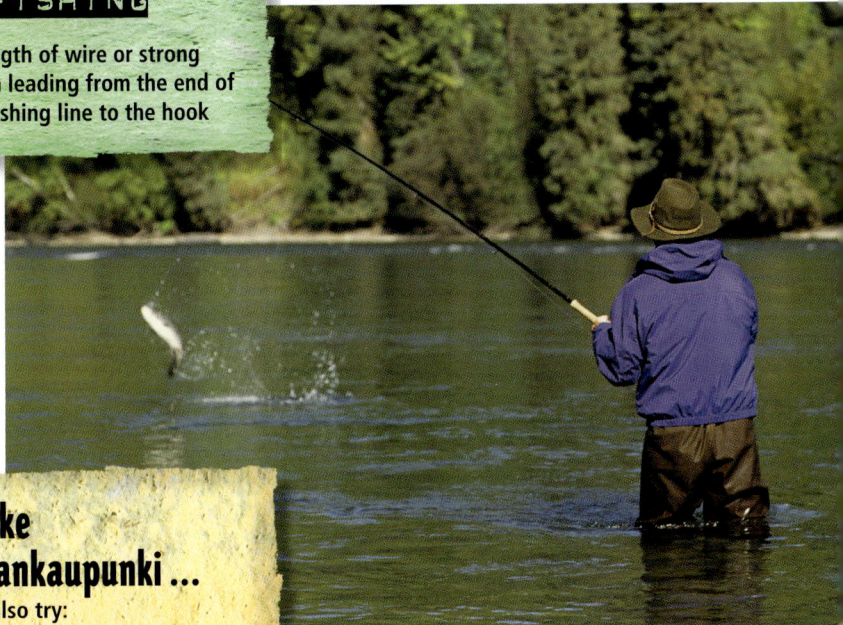

Hooking a fighting fish like a pike is only half the battle. The next steps are to play it and bring it in to the boat or shore.

1. If the fish races off, let out some line. If you try to stop it, the line will probably break.

2. As the fish veers left or right, start to reel it in. This action will pull it steadily toward the boat (or bank).

3. As it gets close to you, the fish may race off again. Let it, then reel it in as in 2, above. The fish will soon get tired enough for you to pull it in close by.

4. Use a net or lip gripper to lift the fish out of the water, and then remove the hook.

The World's Biggest Fish

Some anglers aim to catch fish that put up a good fight. Others go fishing for food and try to catch fish that taste great. But there are a few anglers who just want to go large. In fact, they want to hook the biggest possible fish.

It's hard to tell which one looks more surprised: this 209-pound (95-kilogram) catfish or the man who caught it.

THE WORLD'S BIGGEST FISH
Location: worldwide
Type of fishing: all types
Difficulty level: 5 of 5
Best season: all year round

Tip from a Local
If you're fishing in the Mekong River, bring a strong rod. The river is home to more species of giant freshwater fish than anywhere else.

MEKONG GIANT CATFISH
In 2005 one lucky angler caught a very large Mekong giant catfish. In fact, it was the biggest **freshwater** fish ever caught, anywhere in the world. It weighed an incredible 644.6 pounds (293 kilograms). That's as much as a grizzly bear!

This angler in Brazil has hauled in a whopper of a peacock bass.

THAI GIANT STINGRAY

These giants are found in just a few rivers in Southeast Asia and northern Australia. A 563-pound (256-kilogram) giant stingray was caught in Thailand using a rod and line—the biggest fish ever to be caught that way. It was then released back into the wild.

"CHOY'S MONSTER"

In 1970 a group of anglers off Oahu, Hawaii, landed the largest blue marlin ever caught with a rod and line. It weighed 1,805 pounds (818.7 kilograms). It was named "Choy's Monster" for Cornelius Choy, the skipper of the fishing boat.

Himalaya Mountains

The Himalayas are the world's highest mountains. In spring, melting snow turns to water and comes rushing down from the peaks. The rivers fill with fast-flowing water, crashing its way to the plains thousands of feet below. What a great place to fish!

HIMALAYA MOUNTAINS
Location: India
Type of fishing: river (bank)
Difficulty level: 4.5 of 5
Best season: March to October, but not during **monsoon**

The lakes and fast-flowing rivers of the Himalayas are home to strong, hard-fighting fish. Catching them is a real challenge, even for expert anglers.

FISHING INDIA'S HIMALAYAS

Fast-flowing rivers like these breed strong fish. Strongest of all is your prey: the golden mahseer. Many anglers say this is the most aggressive fish they have ever hooked. The largest mahseer ever caught weighed 121 pounds (55 kilograms). That was many years ago. Today, the effects of overfishing and poaching mean that none of the largest fish survive.

Tip from a Local
Bring some sturdy walking boots. It can be a long hike to reach the fishing spots!

THE SECRET LANGUAGE OF FISHING

monsoon period of very heavy rain in South Asia

fishery area where fish can be caught

If you like the Himalayas ...
you could also try:
- The Rockies, North America
- The Andes, South America

Not many anglers can say they have caught a golden mahseer like this one. These fish are increasingly rare, and most anglers return them to the water after landing them.

ESSENTIAL INFORMATION

The best time to fish for mahseer is before or after the monsoon. During the monsoon itself, **fisheries** are closed.

Fishing equipment: The most exciting way to catch mahseer is by fly fishing or spinning. Take equipment that can cope with heavy fish. You will also need a pair of waders.

Clothing: Pack a long-sleeved shirt, pants, a hat, and sunscreen.

Information: Conserving fish stocks

Many of the world's most popular fish, including the golden mahseer, are becoming endangered. Unless something is done, they may soon die out completely. The mahseer is a good example of what anglers can do to help stop the fall in fish numbers.

• Only take a mahseer's picture home with you, not the actual fish. Once caught, it should be released back into the river.

• Do not fish during the monsoon. Mahseer fisheries are closed because the fish are laying their eggs at this time.

• Once you have caught a golden mahseer, stop fishing. You have already become one of a tiny number of the world's anglers to reel one in. Why be greedy?

Rio Palena

RIO PALENA
Location: northern Patagonia, Chile
Type of fishing: river (bank or boat)
Difficulty level: 4.5 of 5
Best season: November to March

By this stage of your fishing journey around the world, you'll be an expert in just about every kind of fishing. It's time to head for northern Patagonia. Here you'll be rubbing shoulders with Hollywood stars and ex-presidents, in some of the world's most amazing fly-fishing spots.

FISHING RIO PALENA

The waters of Rio Palena come washing down from the **glaciers** in the mountains above. Clean and fast, they are perfect for trout (which were imported to the region in the 1800s). Northern Patagonia is very isolated. Few anglers come here and the rivers are full of fish. Most anglers want to keep things that way, so they use catch-and-release techniques.

THE SECRET LANGUAGE OF FISHING

glacier large, slow-moving "river" of ice and squashed-down snow at the top of a mountain valley

The best season to visit is high summer. During the winter (between June and August) the best fishing spots are snowed in and cannot be reached.

Fishing equipment: A standard 9-foot (2.75-meter) fly rod and medium pound test line will be perfect.

Clothing: Summer days are warm, but at this altitude the sun is very strong. Cover your skin and wear sunscreen. Mountain weather can change fast, so always take a rain jacket and a warm layer.

Tip from a Local

For a change from fishing, visit a rodeo one evening. Most towns hold them twice a month during the summer.

Almost anywhere else in the world, there would probably be a crowd of anglers at a great fishing location like this. In Patagonia, you can fish rivers like this one on your own, if you want to.

If you like Rio Palena ...

you could also try:
• The Falkland Islands, United Kingdom Overseas Territory
• Fiordland National Park, New Zealand

TECHNIQUE

Fishing safety on big, fast-flowing rivers

Like many great trout rivers in the mountains, Rio Palena can be a dangerous place to fish. The waters are fast-flowing and powerful, so anglers who wade in need to be very careful not to be swept away.

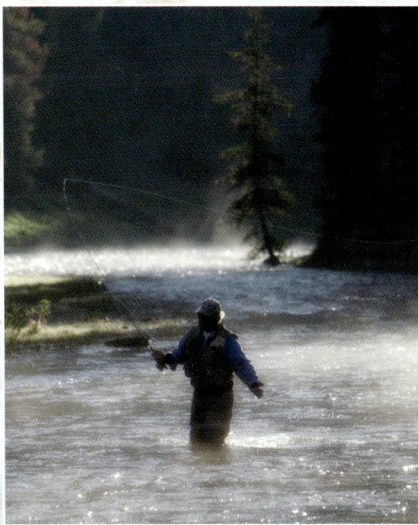

Wearing the right gear will make fishing in fast-flowing water safer and more fun.

• Always wear a flotation vest, ideally one that will self-inflate if you fall into the water.

• Never wade into water where you cannot see the bottom. Murky water can hide holes, slippery rocks, and other hazards that could trip you.

• Carry a cell phone in a sealed waterproof bag. That way, if the worst happens, at least you'll be able to call for help.

Glossary

barb backward-facing spine at the tip of a hook. Barbs can be taken away by filing them off or crushing them flat with a pair of pliers.

breakable able to be pulled apart into smaller pieces. Most fishing rods break into between two and seven pieces, for easy transport.

fishery area where fish can be caught

freshwater living in non-salty water in rivers, lakes and streams

game fish fish that fight hard to escape when hooked

glacier large, slow-moving "river" of ice and squashed-down snow at the top of a mountain valley

lagoon large area of shallow water

lip grippers soft pincers used for gripping a fish's mouth

live bait bait of living (or recently dead) animals, such as worms

loch Scottish lake; in Ireland, known as a lough

lures artificial baits, made of plastic or metal

monsoon period of very heavy rain in South Asia

pound test weight that will break a fishing line

set snag or catch your hook in the fish's mouth

skiff small, wide boat that can float in very shallow water

spit narrow piece of land sticking out into the sea

tackle shop shop selling fishing equipment

trace length of wire or strong nylon leading from the end of the fishing line to the hook

turning tide time when the tide changes direction

OTHER WORDS ANGLERS USE

bivvy domed tent with a large opening at the front, for shelter while night fishing

deadbait bait that is dead

forceps long, thin pliers that can be used to remove a hook from a fish's mouth

match fishing competitive form of coarse fishing

pole fishing fishing using a pole and line, but no reel

quiver tip rod with a very bendy tip, which bends when a fish nibbles on the bait

Finding Out More

THE INTERNET

FactHound offers a safe, fun way to find Internet sites related to this book. All of the sites on FactHound have been researched by our staff.

Here's all you do:
Visit www.facthound.com
FactHound will fetch the best sites for you!

BOOKS FOR YOUNGER READERS

Fishing (Master This!) Martin Ford (PowerKids Press, 2010)

Fishing (Crabtree Contact) Gary Newman (Crabtree Publishing Company, 2009)

Fishing in Lakes and Ponds (Fishing Tips and Techniques) Judy Monroe Peterson (Rosen Central, 2012

MAGAZINES

Most fishing magazines carry a mixture of articles on equipment, personalities, contests, and travel. They all have websites you can locate by searching by name.

Fly Fisherman and *Bassmaster*
These magazines carry high-quality travel articles, features, and equipment reviews, mostly related to fishing in North America.

Index